PIONEER SUMMER

✳ Book One ✳ of the Prairie Skies Series

DEBORAH HOPKINSON

✳

Illustrated by PATRICK FARICY

ALADDIN PAPERBACKS

New York   London   Toronto   Sydney   Singapore

First Aladdin edition May 2002

Text copyright © 2002 by Deborah Hopkinson
Illustrations copyright © 2002 by Patrick Faricy

ALADDIN PAPERBACKS
An imprint of Simon & Schuster
Children's Publishing Division
1230 Avenue of the Americas
New York, NY 10020

Designed by Debra Sfetsios
The text of this book was set in ITC Century Book.
Printed and bound in the United States of America
2 4 6 8 10 9 7 5 3 1
Cataloging-in-Publication Data for the library edition is available
from the Library of Congress.
ISBN 0-689-84349-6 (Aladdin pbk.)

22346

THE KANSAS EMIGRANTS

(To the tune of "Auld Lang Syne")

We cross the prairie, as of old

Our fathers crossed the sea;

To make the West as they the East

The Homestead of the Free.

—John Greenleaf Whittier

ACKNOWLEDGMENTS

I am grateful to historian Paul K. Stuewe for his careful reading of the text and his suggestions for improvement. I'd also like to thank the staff of the Kansas State Historical Society, especially reference librarian Linda Barnickel, who were so helpful both on the phone and in person. Finally, a very special thanks goes out to Michele Hill for tramping through the Kansas tallgrass prairie with me.

For Teresa, Michael, and Angela, with love

�֍

CHAPTER
ONE

When Charlie spied the bird's nest in the branch of the tree, he just had to have it. Even if it meant walking across the thin ice on Polliwog Pond.

"Maybe it's a kingbird's nest, Danny," Charlie told his old black dog. "Grandpa will know for sure."

Charlie Keller loved to collect things—rocks, butterfly wings, pressed flowers, old snake skins, anything.

He especially liked bird's nests. He had eight different kinds, and eight was exactly how old he was. His favorite was a robin's nest, with bits of delicate blue shells still in it. He had a catbird's nest too, and the tiny nest of a sparrow. But not one like this.

The branch with the nest hung far out over Polliwog Pond. Charlie decided he could reach up and grab it if he walked across the ice.

"Stay here, Danny. I'll be right back." Charlie patted

Danny's head. Danny opened his mouth in a big dog smile. His silky black ears twitched. Danny listened to everything Charlie said.

Danny grunted and flopped down in the snow. Lately Danny reminded Charlie of Grandpa. Both walked more slowly these days, and they both loved to take naps. Grandpa fell asleep in his rocker, while Danny liked to curl up on the kitchen rug.

The ice on the pond sparkled in the winter sun. Charlie touched it with his toe. He put one foot down. Then the other. He began to inch across the ice. So far, so good.

Charlie shuffled along, trying not to slip. He kept his dark brown eyes on the nest. Soon he would be close enough to grab it.

Crack! Charlie stopped. What was that?

He looked down. Was the ice about to break? Charlie held his breath. He wanted to run back to shore, but his legs felt like heavy logs.

Suddenly Danny started to bark. Charlie heard a voice calling him. "Charlie. Charlie Keller, where are you?"

Ida Jane. Usually Charlie didn't bother to answer his bossy older sister. But now he yelled, "Over here!"

Ida Jane crashed through the woods. Her bonnet

tilted sideways on her head and her cheeks were bright pink from running.

When Ida Jane saw Charlie, she put both hands on her hips. "Charlie, get back here. That ice might not be safe."

"I—I can't move," sputtered Charlie. "I'm afraid it's going to crack. I'll fall in."

Ida Jane went into action. "Lie down. Spread your weight out," she ordered.

Ida Jane grabbed a large branch from the ground. She threw herself on the snow. She pushed the branch out across the ice. Charlie had to admire that. Ida Jane didn't worry about her skirts, like some girls.

"Wriggle over until you can grab it, Charlie," she said. "I'll pull you to shore."

Carefully Charlie lowered himself flat on the ice. He began to wiggle like a snake. The ice felt wet and cold against his body.

"Come on, faster," urged Ida Jane, reaching out as far as she could.

Suddenly Charlie heard that awful sound again.

Groan! Crack!

"It's giving way!" Charlie cried.

CHAPTER
TWO

"No, you're all right. Just keep coming; you can do it," Ida Jane told him.

Charlie felt his heart pounding. He took a breath. He used his boot to push his body forward. He stretched out his fingers as far as he could.

Slowly, slowly, Charlie inched ahead. The ice held. Closer, closer—there!

Charlie grabbed the branch and shouted. "Got it!"

"Good. Now hold on. I'll pull you." Ida Jane tugged at the branch and Charlie felt himself slide across the ice. His chin scraped against a stone. His wrist hurt from holding on.

"Don't let go," warned Ida Jane. "Almost there!"

At last she reached out and grabbed his arms. Charlie crawled up the bank. They sank down in the wet snow, panting.

Danny stuck his cold nose in Charlie's face. Charlie hugged him tight.

"I think it was a kingbird's nest," he told Ida Jane. "I don't have one."

"You and your collections! Charlie, you know better than to walk on ice this time of year," she scolded. "Winter is almost over."

Charlie sighed. Ida Jane was only ten years old, but it seemed to Charlie that she scolded more than Momma did. Momma said Ida Jane was a bit like a sheepdog. Ida Jane liked herding people.

"Thank you for helping, Ida Jane." Charlie touched his sister's arm. "Please don't tell Momma; she'll just fret."

"Momma!" Ida Jane jumped up. "I almost forgot. We have to get home. Papa wants to talk to us about the meeting."

Charlie scrambled to his feet. "Meeting? What meeting?"

"Don't you remember? He went to hear Mr. Thayer speak last night."

Charlie frowned. "Mr. Thayer?"

Ida Jane shook out her skirts. "Charlie Keller, sometimes I think all those bugs you collect have

7

plugged up your ears. Little Sadie listens better than you do.

"Papa has been talking about Mr. Thayer for weeks," she went on, turning toward home. "Mr. Thayer is the man who wants folks to settle in Kansas. I think Papa has decided to go."

"Papa wouldn't do that! Massachusetts is our home." Charlie skipped to keep up with Ida Jane's sturdy legs. "Besides, Grandpa is here. Papa and Uncle John work in his store."

When they reached the apple trees behind their house, Charlie stopped to wait for Danny, who straggled behind, sniffing his way across the snowy field.

Ida Jane was wrong, Charlie decided. She had to be. Charlie didn't think Danny would want to live in a new, wild place like Kansas. Danny loved their neat white house. He liked exploring the old woods and fields, just as Charlie did.

Danny wouldn't be happy away from home, Charlie thought. And neither would he.

CHAPTER
THREE

Charlie brushed off the dirt as best as he could. He wiped his feet and washed his face. Then he slipped into the parlor. Everyone was waiting. As he tiptoed across the wooden floor, Charlie felt nervous. They hardly ever sat in the parlor.

Sadie was curled up in Momma's lap. Sometimes his little sister reminded Charlie of the wooden tops Grandpa carved. She loved to spin and twirl and run for hours. And when Sadie stopped, she plopped down like a kitten and fell fast asleep.

"Sit down, Son." Papa shifted his long, thin legs so Charlie could get by.

Momma flashed Charlie a smile and patted the chair beside her. Charlie sank into it quickly, hoping she wouldn't notice the wet spots on his clothes.

Sadie sat up and rubbed her eyes. Though she

was just four, Sadie didn't like to miss anything.

Papa cleared his throat. "Children, you know your mother and I are against slavery. We believe it's wrong for one person to own another. We are abolitionists."

"Ab-lishon," murmured Sadie.

Sadie bit her finger and smiled at Charlie, proud of herself. Sadie's smile lit her whole face. Sometimes Papa called her "Sadie Sunshine."

Sadie liked to repeat everything, even if she had no idea what it meant. But Charlie had heard Papa and Momma talk about slavery many times. He knew an abolitionist was a person who wanted to end slavery.

Charlie knew other things about slavery too. He knew that slave families could be torn apart when parents or children were sold away from each other. And he'd heard stories of people trying to escape from slavery only to be caught. Charlie thought he understood why slavery made Papa so angry.

"As America has grown, some people have wanted slavery to spread into our new lands. Others believe this would be wrong," Papa said.

"In 1820 the Congress passed the Missouri Compromise to keep the same number of free states and slave states," he went on. "Congress said Maine would be a free state. Missouri could be a slave state, but other new lands as far north as Missouri would be free."

Papa drew a line in the air as if he were drawing on a real map of the United States. "The Missouri Compromise has helped to keep a balance between slave and free states. But last year the Compromise ended. A new law, the Kansas-Nebraska Act, was passed."

"What does the new law say, Papa?" Ida Jane asked.

"The new law changes everything. Missouri is still a slave state. But the rule about other northern lands being free is gone. Instead, the people in northern territories like Kansas and Nebraska will decide about slavery themselves."

Charlie frowned. "I'm not sure I understand, Papa."

"Someday Kansas will become a state, Charlie. If the people there want it to be a free state, they can vote against slavery."

"What if more people in Kansas vote for slavery?" asked Ida Jane.

"Then Kansas would become a slave state," Momma told her. "And slavery would keep spreading farther west."

Suddenly Papa pounded his fist on his knee. "We must not let that happen. That's why a man named Eli Thayer is helping people settle in Kansas."

"But, Papa, why do we care about Kansas?" asked Charlie. "We live here."

"Charlie, I have searched my heart. I feel we must do something to stop slavery from spreading," exclaimed Papa. "We leave for Kansas in early April. By summer, we'll be pioneers."

Leave in April! Charlie's mouth fell open. Ida Jane had been right, after all.

"But, but . . . Papa, this is our home," stammered Charlie. "Besides, I—I don't think Danny will like Kansas."

Momma put her hand on his shoulder. "Charlie, there are wolves in Kansas. Kansas is too dangerous for an old dog who can't run fast anymore."

Papa nodded. "I'm sure Grandpa will be happy to keep Danny, Son."

All at once Charlie felt cold everywhere, almost as if he *had* fallen through the ice. He swallowed hard.

"You mean Grandpa isn't coming either? And I can't take Danny?" Charlie tried to blink back the tears that rushed to his eyes. "Then I don't want to go to Kansas, either."

CHAPTER
FOUR

Click, click, chug. Click, click, chug.

Rattle, rattle. Click, click, chug.

Charlie tried to see out the train window, but it was too dark. He frowned and rubbed his head to make it stop hurting.

"I wish you wouldn't mope," hissed Ida Jane from the seat across from him.

"I'm not moping. I'm just tired of this dirty train."

The train *was* dirty. At first Momma had sent Charlie to the water tank at the end of the car with napkins from their food basket. He wet them so they could wipe their faces and hands. So much soot and dust had come off that their napkins turned black.

But now Charlie felt too tired to care that he was grimy and rumpled. He didn't think Momma cared

13

anymore either. She was dozing next to Ida Jane with Sadie in her lap.

Sadie was sleeping, at last. But Charlie knew that in the morning she would want him to hold her hand so she could walk up and down the aisle and wave to everyone. Again. And again.

"Where are we, anyway?" Charlie asked Ida Jane crossly. Since getting on the train in Boston, they'd gone through Albany, Cleveland, and Chicago. They had passed new green pastures, young calves, and farmers planting corn.

Ida Jane shrugged. "In Illinois, I think. Papa says we should reach Alton in the morning. Alton's on the Missouri border and we'll get a boat to St. Louis there. Just think, a real steamboat!"

Charlie shrugged. He just wanted to get off this train. His neck was sore. His legs felt cramped. His new boots pinched. He was almost too tired to feel sad.

Ida Jane leaned forward. "Aren't you excited at all, Charlie? Just think, everything we see is new."

Charlie didn't answer. He leaned his head against the window and closed his eyes. A picture of Grandpa and Danny came into his mind.

"I'm not like you and Papa," Charlie wanted to

tell Ida Jane. *"I didn't want anything to change."*

But it seemed to Charlie that Papa had talked of nothing but change and their new life ever since that day in the parlor.

"Just think, Kansas!" Papa had exclaimed almost every day. "And settling there will be easy for us, thanks to Mr. Thayer and his friends. They've formed a special organization, called the New England Emigrant Aid Company, to help us get cheaper train and boat tickets."

Ever since they'd been on the train, Papa had spent long hours huddled with the other men headed west. He'd asked lots of questions about farming. Back home, Papa had worked in Grandpa's store. Now he had his heart set on being a farmer. Charlie just hoped Papa would know what to do.

Papa sank into the seat beside Charlie. "Still awake, Son?"

Charlie wanted to pretend he was looking out the window. But in the dark, all he could see in the window was the reflection of his own thin face.

Papa grinned. He didn't seem to notice that Charlie didn't smile back.

"We'll be off the train tomorrow, Charlie," Papa said cheerfully. "The boat ride to St. Louis is only about twenty miles. We'll stop to buy supplies there, then take a long steamboat ride to Kansas City."

Papa put his hand on Charlie's knee. "Have you been writing in that journal Grandpa gave you?"

"It's not like a diary, Papa," said Charlie, shaking his head. "Grandpa wants me to write about plants and birds and insects. He says that's how men of science do it. And he wants me to tell him all about Kansas."

"He'll like that, I'm sure. Why, I bet he'll even read your letters out loud to Danny." Papa patted Charlie's shoulder. "Try to sleep now."

Charlie curled up against the window. The train rocked and chugged and bumped through the night. In a way, Charlie thought, the chug was the train's heartbeat.

Sometimes, when he was little, Charlie used to fall asleep with his head against Danny's warm, sleek sides. Danny's heartbeat was quick and strong then. Charlie wondered what Danny was doing now.

"Don't you worry about Danny. This old dog and I, we belong together, Charlie," Grandpa had told him.

"He'll miss me," Charlie had said. "He'll think I left because I didn't love him anymore."

At that, Grandpa had put both hands on Charlie's shoulders and looked into his eyes. "Don't you fret about that, Charlie Keller. Danny and me, we understand that you have to go."

Grandpa pulled Charlie close. "I hear they've got big skies out there in Kansas Territory. But it's the same sky that covers us here. If you ask me, the sky's a lot like love. It just spreads out over folks no matter how far apart they are."

After a while the rumble of the train put Charlie to sleep. He dreamed he was curled up with Grandpa in his rocking chair, old Danny at their feet.

CHAPTER
FIVE

Charlie was leaning far over the railing of the steamboat when he felt a poke in his ribs. He jumped.

"Hey, watch out!" he cried, grabbing hold of the rail.

"Did I scare you? I've been watching you. You're a Yankee, aren't you?" asked a skinny girl in a blue sunbonnet. She didn't stop to hear his answer. "I bet you're moving to Kansas. My daddy says you Yankees are going there to cause trouble."

A Yankee! No one had ever called him a Yankee before. Charlie peered at the girl. She had a long, reddish yellow braid and a sprinkle of freckles on her cheeks.

"My family doesn't want trouble," he mumbled softly, shading his eyes against the bright Missouri sun.

The girl shrugged. "Sometimes I think the only reason we're moving to Kansas is 'cause Daddy doesn't like home anymore. Not since Mama died of cholera last year."

Charlie looked over at the girl. She was staring into the dark waters below.

"It surely was awful," she whispered, almost to herself. "Mama was so thirsty. Her eyes got hollow as an old log."

Charlie tried to think what to say. Ida Jane would have asked the girl more, but all he could do was stand still.

Thump! Scrape! What was that? Charlie grabbed the rail tighter.

The girl pointed to the river. She seemed to forget her sadness. "Oh, we've hit a big sand bar. Now the sailors have to get us away from it. If we get stuck we'll *never* get off Big Muddy."

"Big Muddy?"

"Silly, that's what we call the Missouri River," she laughed, crinkling up her nose. "One time my daddy put an egg in a glass of river water. The water was so brown I couldn't even see the egg through the glass."

The girl turned to stare at him. Her eyes were the same blue as a robin's egg, Charlie thought.

"What's your name, anyway?" she asked.

"I'm Charlie Keller, from Massachusetts."

"Pleased to meet you, Massachusetts Charlie. I'm Florinda Morgan, from Missouri," she declared. "You can call me Flory. Everyone does."

Charlie and Flory leaned over the railing as far as they dared. Below them, Charlie could hear the first mate ordering the other sailors. "Stoke the fire. Let's get 'er clear!"

Thick smoke rolled from the smokestack. The boat lurched back toward the middle of the river.

Charlie watched two sailors drop a heavy weight into the water. "What are they doing?"

"That's called 'sounding,'" Flory told Charlie. "They're checking to see how deep the water is."

The sailors yelled up cheerfully, "Four feet large!"

"Hurrah! That means we're in deeper water. They did it!" Flory cried.

Charlie and Flory clapped. Below them, the sailors heard their cheer and waved their caps.

Charlie felt someone grab his arm. Ida Jane stood over him, frowning.

"Charlie, what are you doing here?" Ida Jane glared at Flory until she skipped away, her shiny braid bouncing down her back.

"Charlie, that girl sounded like she was from the South. Papa might not like you talking to her," his sister scolded. "What if her family owns slaves?"

Charlie frowned. Papa had always talked about slave owners as bad people. But Flory had seemed nice.

"There *are* slave owners on this boat, you know. Slaves, too—even children." Ida Jane leaned close. "Why, there's a boy your age and a little girl no bigger than Sadie."

Charlie nodded. "I saw them this morning too. Papa had words with the slave owner, Mr. Johnson."

"What happened?" asked Ida Jane, her eyes wide.

"They got into an argument about Kansas," Charlie said. "Papa said Mr. Johnson might as well give up now, 'cause we New England folks were going to make Kansas free."

Charlie was glad Papa hadn't gotten into a real fight. Mr. Johnson was a big, hefty man, but Papa was thin, just like Charlie. Momma called them her two string beans.

"Did Papa win the argument?" Ida Jane wanted to know.

Charlie shrugged. "I don't know. Momma sent me out here. But she stayed in the dining room with Sadie. She's afraid to bring Sadie on deck."

"No wonder! It would be just like Sadie to squirm out of Momma's arms and fall right into the Missouri River," Ida Jane said.

Charlie looked over the edge. He wouldn't want to feel that muddy water close over his head. He had never seen a river so wide before.

"You better not fall in. I might not be there to help you," said Ida Jane with a grin.

"The gong's about to sound for dinner," she added, turning to go. "Don't be late or you won't get a seat for the first serving."

Momma said steamboats were sometimes called "floating palaces" because the food was so good. There were three hundred people on board their boat, yet the cooks made a feast every night. Charlie had never seen so much food—meat and fish, fruit, nuts, cakes and candies. The tables had room for only seventy-five people at a time, so the men had to wait their turns, while ladies and children ate first. The table was cleared and set again four times.

Gong! The dinner bell began to ring. Momma would be mad if he were late.

Charlie pounded across the deck. He turned the corner.

Thump! Bump! Charlie collided hard with a little girl. He put his hands out to keep her from falling. But it was too late.

He had knocked her down.

CHAPTER
SIX

"Mama!" The girl began to wail in a high, scared voice.

Charlie knelt beside her. "I'm sorry."

Charlie stared. This was the little girl from the slave family.

The girl was thin. Her skin made him think of warm cocoa on a winter afternoon. He wanted to touch her arm.

She's so small, Charlie thought. How could anyone make a tiny child be a slave?

"Are you hurt?" Charlie asked softly. "Do you want to go to your mama?"

The little girl sniffed. She fixed him with enormous brown eyes. Her bottom lip trembled.

"Jennie," someone called. "Jennie, come here."

Charlie glanced up. The girl's brother stood not far away, staring hard at Charlie.

Jennie jumped up. Her bare feet made a slap-slap-slapping sound on the smooth deck. She ran fast, her light cotton dress swinging around her legs.

The boy grabbed his little sister's hand. Jennie turned back once to look at Charlie. Almost, Charlie thought, as if she were afraid he would chase after her.

After dinner the dining room bustled with music and card games. But soon mattresses were put down, and everyone rushed to find a place for the night. Some people were lucky enough to sleep in state-rooms, but many had to stay in the main cabin.

The Kellers had a corner near the door. When Momma gave Charlie a kiss good night she felt his forehead. "You're always my quiet one, Charlie. But on this journey you've hardly said a word. Are you feeling well?"

"I'm fine." Charlie loved Momma's soft touch. It was like being brushed with rose petals.

"Momma, I wanted to ask you . . ." Charlie whispered, trying to find the words. "I know you and Papa are against slavery . . ."

Momma nodded, her face still close to his. "Yes, of course. That's what it means to be an abolitionist."

"Am I old enough to be one too?" Charlie wondered.

"If that is what your heart tells you."

"But Momma, if I *am* an abolitionist, does that mean I must hate people from the South?"

Momma smiled. "I hope you never hate anyone, dear boy. We must be charitable, and help people see their errors." She kissed him on the forehead. "Now go to sleep. Tomorrow we'll be in Kansas City."

It wasn't safe to travel on the shallow river after dark, so the steamboat was tied up to a large tree on shore. The river lapped at its great sides, and it rocked gently, up and down, up and down.

Soft sighs from the other sleepers floated around Charlie. But the rocking of the boat kept him awake a long time. He couldn't help thinking about Flory Morgan, who had lost her mama. And about little Jennie, who could be sold away from hers.

CHAPTER
SEVEN

Kansas City! Charlie was glad when the town came into sight along the river's edge. He was tired of traveling—nearly four days on the dusty train and five more on the crowded steamer. He couldn't wait to get off the boat!

"It looks like a beehive, Momma. Everyone is moving at once," Ida Jane cried as the levee came into view.

Momma nodded, holding Sadie's hand tightly so she wouldn't climb on the railing or dart away. "What a busy place! Look at how strong those men are. They're unloading barrels of flour as easy as if they were tossing feather pillows."

"See the big horsies!" hollered Sadie, her eyes wide and sparkling.

Charlie pointed. "And look there, Sadie! Wagons and plows and stoves and hundreds of bags of seed."

"Our supplies will be unloaded soon too," Papa told them. "I bought a breaking plow when we stopped in St. Louis. I'll have to see about getting a wagon and ox team here. We'll stay in a hotel until everything is ready. Then we'll head to Lawrence and I'll set out to look for a claim."

Momma smiled. "With any luck, we'll have some sort of roof over our heads before the summer is over, even if it's made of prairie grass."

"This is the American Hotel," Papa said, pointing proudly to a large, four-story brick building. "It's owned by Mr. Thayer's group, the New England Emigrant Aid Company. Why, they say the restaurant can seat one hundred and fifty people! The company bought it so free-state folks like us would have a safe place to stay. Kansas City is still in the slave state of Missouri, after all."

Charlie looked around nervously. But so far, except for the man on the boat Papa had argued with, everyone had been friendly.

Ida Jane whispered to Charlie, "I heard one man say folks like us won't last. He called us 'soft-slippered.'"

"Soft-slippered? What does that mean?"

"I guess he doesn't believe we're strong enough for the Kansas prairie. He thinks we'll just give up, go home and put on our slippers." Ida Jane tossed her chin in the air. "As for me, I plan to stay in Kansas until I'm eighty."

"How do you know?" Charlie wondered. "You haven't even seen the Territory yet."

Sometimes Charlie just couldn't understand Ida Jane. Didn't she miss home like he did? Didn't she think about it at all?

"Now don't forget to buy flour," Momma reminded Papa next morning, as he set out to get more supplies.

"Yes, and we need more tools, like hatchets, a hand saw, and a sledge hammer. Let's see, what else?" Papa checked the list he'd been working on for weeks. "A keg of lard and one of molasses, some potatoes, and two bushels of seed corn."

Papa is like Ida Jane, Charlie decided. *He's happiest looking ahead, never back.* But when Papa returned later, Charlie saw a worried look on his thin face for the first time. Papa seemed tired, too.

"Potatoes were high, about a dollar a bushel. Not

only that, I hear they're five dollars once we get into the Territory," Papa said with a sigh. "Cornmeal cost a dollar for a fifty-pound sack. The only thing I could get cheap was apples, and even then I had to pay fifty cents for a bushel basket."

"Did you get my wheat flour?" asked Momma.

Papa shook his head. "No, it was simply too dear. We'll have to get used to eating cornmeal instead."

"What about oxen, Papa? Did you buy a team and a wagon?" Ida Jane wanted to know.

"I did indeed. And tomorrow you will see them," Papa told them. "We're almost there. Tomorrow we'll set foot in Kansas at last."

But the next morning when Charlie awoke, he knew right away something was wrong. Momma was sitting by Papa's side, wiping his forehead with a wet cloth.

"What's the matter?" whispered Charlie, rubbing his eyes.

Momma swallowed hard. Her voice trembled a little. "Papa is sick. Very sick."

CHAPTER
EIGHT

"Perhaps it's because of the poor water we had to drink on that steamboat," Momma went on in a low voice. "Why, sometimes I think they just took the water up right from the river. I surely hope it's not the cholera."

Cholera! Charlie felt his stomach lurch. Papa lay so still and quiet. Charlie bit his lip to keep from crying.

Ida Jane was awake now too. She whispered, "Momma, I heard people on the steamer say there was a cholera epidemic in Missouri just last year."

Papa just couldn't have cholera, Charlie thought. Most people who got cholera didn't get better. He remembered Flory, and how she had looked when she talked about her mama.

"Papa just *has* to get better," Charlie said fiercely.

Momma put her arms around both of them. "We will pray that Papa gets well soon. But when he does, children, we'll have to go on alone. The other families who came on the train with us will be leaving for Kansas Territory today."

"Why can't they wait for us?" demanded Ida Jane.

"It's too expensive to stay in this hotel," Momma explained. "Why, it costs three dollars and fifty cents a week. We'll try to catch up with them as soon as Papa gets better."

Charlie hugged his mother hard.

"Now, don't fret, Charlie and Ida Jane," said Momma, forcing herself to smile. "I am a good nurse. But I need your help. You must help watch Sadie while I tend to Papa. She's so high-spirited it's hard to keep her quiet."

Ida Jane nodded. "We'll take her downstairs where we can visit with other people. That way she won't be a bother and Papa can rest."

Sadie was awake now. She jumped up, pouted and stamped her foot. "I am *not* a bother, Ida Jane!"

When they were dressed, Charlie and Ida Jane each grabbed one of Sadie's hands.

"Shh. Papa is sleeping. We can go downstairs, eat

breakfast, and look out the windows," Charlie told her. "We'll see lots of horses, Sadie."

Sadie loved animals almost as much as Charlie did. Her favorites were horses and chickens.

"Papa just has to get well, Charlie," Ida Jane whispered as they walked down the hall with Sadie between them.

Charlie was silent. None of this would have happened if they had stayed home in Massachusetts. Home where they belonged.

It wasn't easy to keep Sadie out of trouble. Charlie decided that what Sadie loved most was to make her big sister and brother run after her.

The first day went fine, but Papa was still sick the next afternoon. Ida Jane and Charlie had run out of ideas. They had played every game they could think of with Sadie, and she still wouldn't take a nap.

A large party of settlers arrived in the hotel, loaded down with trunks and boxes and crates of supplies.

"Are you moving to Kansas too?" asked a boy about Charlie's age.

"Yes, we're leaving for the Territory soon."

"I can't wait," said the boy excitedly. "My pa's gonna teach me to shoot rabbits and wild turkeys."

Charlie wondered if Papa would get well and be able to teach him to shoot too.

Ida Jane pulled at Charlie's arm. "Charlie, where is she?"

"Who?"

"Sadie, of course," cried Ida Jane, tugging nervously at her braids. "Sadie has disappeared!"

CHAPTER
NINE

Charlie looked around. "I thought she was sitting with you."

Ida Jane ran to the window. "No, I thought you were watching her while I ran upstairs to check on Papa and bring Momma some tea."

Charlie thought a minute. "She might be in the hotel somewhere. But what if she went outside to look at horses? I'd better search for her before she wanders too far."

Ida Jane hesitated. "Momma wouldn't like you going outside."

"But I have to, Ida Jane."

"All right. Be careful," she warned, turning so fast her skirt whirled. "I'll look around inside the hotel."

Charlie ran out the door. The street bustled with people, animals, wagons, and carts.

"Sadie!" he shouted. "Sadie Keller, where are you?"

He dashed to one corner and looked down the road. No Sadie.

"Hey, watch out!" someone yelled. Charlie jumped back out of the way of a man on a large black horse.

"Sadie!" he cried, almost desperate now. Sadie could get knocked down and killed here. She wasn't used to such commotion.

Charlie had never seen a town this busy. Men led cows on ropes, calves trotting behind. People shouted and ponies neighed. Wagons rolled by. Fat chickens squawked, bumping along in boxes tied onto the backs of carts.

Charlie walked down the street clenching his fists. Where could she be? What would Momma do if Sadie got hurt?

And then above the clamor he heard a shout. "Massachusetts Charlie!"

Charlie could not believe his eyes. Coming down the road was a large wagon, pulled by a fine team of oxen. A man led the team and there on the wagon seat perched Flory Morgan—and Sadie!

"This little wanderer belong to you, young man?" Flory's father called out as he halted the oxen.

"Yes, thank you, sir." Charlie rushed up to the wagon and let his breath out all at once. "Papa is sick and Momma is taking care of him in the hotel. Somehow Sadie got loose."

Mr. Morgan grinned. "I had a cow like that once. Seems to me her name was Sadie too."

Mr. Morgan lifted Sadie to the ground. Charlie grabbed hold of her hand. Sadie squeezed tight and stared down at her little toes. Her face was red and Charlie could see tears on her eyelashes. Charlie put his arm around her.

"You're safe now, Sadie Sunshine," he whispered.

"I recognized Sadie from the boat," Flory told him. "Right away I knew she was your sister. She hadn't gone far, just around the corner. And she didn't get hurt or nothing. Daddy figured you might be at this Yankee hotel."

"Are you heading into the Territory today?" Charlie asked.

Flory nodded. "Daddy says we'll settle near Franklin, where there are other folks from Missouri." She grinned. "Well, good-bye, Massachusetts Charlie. Maybe we'll see each other again."

Charlie waved until the Morgans turned the corner.

I don't care what Ida Jane says, Charlie thought, *I like Flory Morgan. Even if she is from Missouri.*

Momma *was* a good nurse, and by the end of the third day Papa could sit up, though his face was white as a winter moon.

"I'll be fine in the morning, Sarah," he insisted.

"James, I'm worried. I know you have your heart set on farming," answered Momma, tucking a blanket around him. "But you're not a strong man. Perhaps a store would be better."

"Sarah, being a storekeeper is what my father and brother liked. But I'm not like Dad or John. I want to try something new."

Papa took Momma's hand. "The prairie air will make me strong, and the children will help," he said softly. "This is our chance to have our own piece of land."

Papa looked over at Charlie. "Besides, we need to do our part to make Kansas a free state. Right, Charlie?"

Charlie ducked his head and nodded. What if Papa guessed he just wanted to be home with Grandpa and Danny? And what would Papa say if he found out Charlie's only friend so far was a girl from Missouri?

CHAPTER
TEN

"What a glorious spring day," Momma said happily, as they left the bustle of Kansas City behind. "It's warmer than New England in April."

"Where are we headed next?" Ida Jane asked, walking side by side with Papa.

"To the free-soil town of Lawrence," replied Papa. "This is Shawnee country. We'll camp near a cabin owned by an Indian who runs a sort of boarding house."

"Will we see many Indians near us, Papa?" asked Charlie. Grandpa had told him Indians knew a lot about plants and birds.

"Some, but many have already been pushed farther west," Papa said. Charlie thought about that. He wondered if they had felt as sad leaving home as he did.

44

The sun warmed Charlie's back. He walked beside the oxen, listening to the creaking leather of the harness. He breathed in the scent of damp earth and sweet blossoms.

The road snaked up and down gentle, rolling hills covered with fresh grass. Clusters of trees clung to the creek bottoms. Papa said he recognized wild plums, crab apples, and cottonwoods.

Charlie lost count of the hawks he saw.

Flap, glide, flap, glide. Sometimes they hung so still in the air Charlie thought they must be tied to clouds by invisible ribbons.

But what surprised Charlie most was the sky.

"Back home we see the sky in patches, between the trees," he said to Momma when they stopped so Papa could rest and they could all eat biscuits. "It's different here."

"Prairie skies," said Momma softly. "We're so far from the sea, but this land and sky somehow put me in mind of it."

She patted his arm. "I know you miss home, Charlie. I try to keep Grandpa and Danny in my heart every day too. But Papa is right. We must follow our beliefs."

Charlie stared ahead, to a line where the sky and the earth seemed to meet.

"I hope you'll come to like some things about Kansas, Charlie," Momma added. "Maybe you can start by liking the sky."

Charlie took a bite of biscuit and dried beef. This prairie sky *was* big, just as Grandpa had said it would be. Grandpa had also said the sky was like love, spreading out over folks no matter how far apart they were.

Charlie looked up and tried to imagine Grandpa and Danny, taking a walk in the fields together. Maybe, he thought, they were looking up at a bright blue sky right now.

CHAPTER
ELEVEN

"Well, I will surely be glad to leave this place," said Momma crossly. "It's certainly not a proper hotel. The mattresses are full of fleas and bedbugs."

Papa had been gone for four days. He'd left them in Lawrence to look for a claim near the other New England families.

Momma had expected a hotel like the one in Kansas City. But Lawrence was a new town. There were only about fifty cabins made of logs and rough boards. Some of the buildings were no more than "hay tents," two rows of poles joined together at the top and covered with prairie hay.

"At least we don't have to worry about Sadie getting run over on the busy street," said Ida Jane to Charlie one morning.

"I never told Momma or Papa about her getting

lost, did you?" Charlie asked her.

Ida Jane shook her head so hard her bonnet tipped sideways. "No! And I hope we never have to. Momma worries enough as it is."

"I've found us a claim just south of here," cried Papa happily, when he returned a few days later. "We'll call it Spring Creek, after the creek that's there."

Momma jumped up to greet him. "Did you find the other families from New England?"

"Well, no," Papa admitted, lowering his pack to the floor. "It seems they've scattered into the Territory."

A frown flashed across Momma's forehead. "But James, the talk here in Lawrence is how much trouble everyone expects with men from Missouri. They're calling them 'border ruffians.'"

She took Papa's coat. "Will we be safe if we're not in with free-soil people?"

"We won't be far from Lawrence," Papa assured her, sitting down to take off his boots and rub his sore feet. "We are near Franklin, which *is* a proslavery town. But it's small, and I'm sure we'll be just fine."

Charlie jumped. Franklin! That's where Flory

49

Morgan had been headed. Maybe he would see her again someday.

Momma had managed to buy a rooster and three hens in Lawrence. On the day they left for Spring Creek, she put them carefully into a wooden crate in the back of the wagon.

Momma shook her finger at Sadie. "Sadie, you are not to take them out of their box. If they get loose, we shall have no eggs to eat or to sell!"

"Yes, Momma," said Sadie, staring up at a pretty red hen.

"Come on, Sadie, you can pat the new calf," said Ida Jane. "We're almost ready!"

Charlie knew Momma was fretting about money, but she had been firm about one thing. They needed a cow. Momma had found this cow and calf for a good price. She bought them from a woman whose husband and baby had died of fever. The woman was selling everything and heading back home to Ohio.

"I wish you better luck than I've had," the woman had told Momma. She paused and patted the cow one last time. "Her name's Annie."

*

"What's Spring Creek like, Papa?" Ida Jane asked as they headed out.

"The creek has some cottonwoods and other trees strung along it. Enough to make a cabin," said Papa, guiding the oxen up a low hill. "There's a sweep of bluestem prairie grass, dotted with wildflowers. The grass is low now, but this summer it will grow higher than your head. And we have a nice hill to the west."

"How's the soil?" asked Charlie.

"The soil is as rich and brown as your eyes," said Papa with a laugh.

They reached Spring Creek in the afternoon and slept that night under the wagon. The next morning the sound of a bird woke Charlie.

He slipped out of his blankets and pulled on his boots. Then he scurried to the top of the small hill Papa had told them about. From here, the prairie rolled out softly in every direction. The grass waved and the wind made music in it.

Charlie let out a long breath. He had never imagined it would be like this.

He lay flat on the grass and looked up. The only thing in the world was the bright prairie sky.

CHAPTER
TWELVE

"Charlie, Momma wants you to fetch water like she asked, not look at wildflowers!" scolded Ida Jane one hot summer morning. She straightened her bonnet and headed out to weed Momma's vegetable plants.

Charlie waited until she was out of sight. Then he picked the bright purple flower and stuck it in his pocket anyway.

Charlie wished he had time to press it into his journal to send to Grandpa. But since coming to Spring Creek, he hadn't had a chance to write to Grandpa even once. There was too much work. These days Momma even gave Sadie chores to do.

Charlie picked up the yoke and buckets. Papa had made a yoke that fit across the shoulders, and on either end was a bucket. When the buckets were full, the edges of the yoke cut into Charlie's shoulders.

Charlie thought fetching water was the hardest chore. After he was done, it would be time to walk to the creek and look for sticks and brush for fuel. Then he'd go to where Papa was breaking the sod and help him, or weed the young corn.

Summer had been Charlie's favorite time back home. But now it seemed that summer was just a time to worry about winter. That was all Momma and Papa talked about.

Would they grow enough food? If they ran out of supplies, would they have enough money to buy more? Could Papa get the cabin finished and the walls chinked before the weather turned?

Momma had hoped to have a real roof over her head by now, but they were still sleeping under the wagon. "Planting comes first," Papa said.

Papa was up at first light each morning. But turning the prairie sod was hard work. The grass was so thick that sometimes when the wind was calm, Papa burned off small sections of a field to make it easier to plow.

Papa had done that yesterday. He was getting a field ready to plant corn for next spring. He'd already put in pumpkins, squashes, tomatoes, beans, potatoes, and cucumbers. But corn would be their mainstay.

"Corn grows well here," Papa had told them. "We can depend on it."

But Charlie was already sick of it. It seemed to him that Momma made everything out of corn—cornbread, corn grits, corn pudding and johnny-cakes. Charlie couldn't help missing the taste of bread made of flour, the kind Momma used to bake back home.

After he had filled the buckets, Charlie moved slowly through the tall grass. The water made a sloshing sound every time he took a step.

He stopped to catch his breath. He looked around him. He saw something move out of the corner of his eye. What was it?

He stared. There was an animal in the grass, he was sure of it.

Charlie felt his heart beat hard. He held his breath. What kind of creature could it be? A coyote? A wolf?

Charlie got ready to run.

Then the creature made a noise.

"Woof!"

Charlie's mouth dropped open.

The noise came again. "Woof!"

A dog! Charlie was sure of it.

Carefully Charlie set down the yoke and the buckets. He pushed the grass aside and peered closely.

At first he didn't see anything.

And then, there he was.

He was the skinniest dog Charlie had ever seen. He was almost the same color as the dry, golden grass. His ribs poked through his scraggy coat. His tail drooped between his legs.

The dog cowered low and whined softly.

"Don't be afraid, boy," Charlie crooned. "I'm your friend."

The dog cocked his head at Charlie. His tail began to thump weakly.

Charlie stooped down slowly and put his hand out. He's not even full grown, Charlie realized. "How did you get here, pup? Did you get lost from a wagon on the California trail?"

Charlie reached back into one of the pails and cupped some water into his hands. "Hey, boy," he whispered. "Want a drink?"

Charlie crept closer to the pup, who watched with big amber eyes. "You're just the color of a lion, aren't you?" said Charlie softly. "Come on, Lion, have a drink."

At first Lion shivered and whined with fear. But soon he put his muzzle into Charlie's hands and lapped up the water noisily.

After a few minutes more, Charlie coaxed Lion into his lap. The dog burrowed his head under Charlie's arm.

Charlie laughed. "Poor thing. I don't think you would've lasted much longer out here. Come on, let's go home."

But now Charlie realized he couldn't carry Lion and the water at the same time. He had to hold the yoke steady on his shoulders or it would fall off. And he didn't dare go back to camp without water.

Charlie had an idea. Reaching into his pocket, he pulled out a biscuit. He put the dog on the ground and let him sniff the biscuit in his hand. Then he broke off a piece and fed it to him. Lion crunched it eagerly.

"Follow me, boy, and you can have the rest."

Charlie stood and loaded the yoke on his shoulders.

"Come on, Lion," he called. "Let's go home."

Walk three steps. Stop and call. Keep walking some more. Charlie inched closer to home. Whenever he stopped to look, Lion was two steps behind him.

"Good boy," he cried.

Charlie came around a bend and stopped.

Something pricked at his nose. He wasn't sure how long the smell had been there. He stopped and looked over the tall prairie grass. Nothing behind him, nothing in front.

Then to his right he saw it. Smoke! A thin line of fire in the grass, near where Papa had burned yesterday. Had a spark remained smoldering?

The wind swished across the grass. Papa had told them how dangerous a prairie fire could be. Especially this time of year, when the tall grass stood parched and dry.

The fire was still small. But the wind could make it bigger any minute.

He stood frozen. More than anything, Charlie wanted to pick Lion up and run to safety. What if Lion got caught in the fire? What if he got scared and ran off forever?

But Charlie knew he had to take the yoke and

buckets with him. He couldn't drop them and take the chance of the fire spreading fast and burning them. His family depended on these buckets for water. No, Charlie couldn't leave them behind.

Charlie would have to run and carry the yoke at the same time. He looked at Lion. But that meant he couldn't carry Lion, too.

Would Lion follow him to safety?

CHAPTER
✳THIRTEEN✳

Charlie took off, pushing through the tall prairie grass. He steadied the yoke on his shoulders as best he could.

"Come on, boy," he called. "I have to run and warn Papa. Now! I can't wait up for you."

Charlie hoped with all his heart that Lion would follow. At first he saw Lion's brown head bobbing behind him. But the next time Charlie looked back, all he saw was grass.

If only he could drop the buckets and go back for Lion! Charlie panted hard. Sweat dripped into his eyes and made them burn.

But he didn't dare waste another second. He couldn't let Papa's hard work burn up. He couldn't let the fire destroy his new home.

At last Charlie caught sight of Papa. Charlie yelled, "Papa! Over here! Fire!"

At first Charlie thought Papa couldn't hear him. Then Papa straightened up and began to run. His long legs reminded Charlie of a grasshopper.

"It's over there!" Charlie hollered, pointing.

Papa didn't stop. "Get to the wagon. It's too far from the creek to put out with water. Tell Momma to bring blankets and shovels."

The next hour seemed like a blur to Charlie.

He had never seen Momma look so fierce. She threw off her bonnet and apron. Her hair came loose from its neat bun and streamed down her back. She yelled and beat back the fire as hard as she could.

While Momma and Papa tried to smother the flames, Charlie and Ida Jane worked at digging a trench between their half-built cabin and the fire. Then Papa burned the prairie grass and fanned the flames to meet the wildfire.

At last the fire had nowhere to go. They had beaten it back until nothing was left but a patch of black, smoky stubble.

"Thank goodness the wind only came in puffs today," said Momma, wiping dark soot from her forehead with the edge of her skirt.

"More than that," said Papa, "we're lucky Charlie is always looking so carefully into the grass for birds and bugs. If he hadn't seen it when he did, in another hour or two it would have been too big for us."

Ida Jane poked Charlie gently in the ribs. "Thanks, Charlie."

"Where's Sadie?" asked Papa suddenly.

"Safe at the wagon, keeping watch over Annie, the calf, and the chickens. I warned her that if she moved, I wouldn't give her a chick when the eggs hatch," said Momma. "Sadie loves those chickens. If anything can keep her from wandering, they can."

Wandering! Suddenly Charlie gasped. Where was Lion? Had all the noise and shouting scared him away?

"Charlie, what's the matter?" asked Momma.

"Just before the fire, I found a dog," Charlie gulped. "He's still a puppy. Maybe he got lost from a wagon heading to California."

Momma frowned. "Was he tame?"

Charlie nodded. "He was weak and thin. I wanted to carry him, but I couldn't, not with the yoke and buckets. He was the color of a lion. That's what I call him. 'Lion.' Maybe the fire scared him away." Charlie felt his throat get tight. "I'm afraid he won't come back."

Papa and Momma looked at each other.

Momma said, "Ida Jane, we must go check on Sadie and get supper started. Come."

"But . . ." began Ida Jane.

Momma pulled Ida Jane up the path.

When they were alone, Papa put his arm over Charlie's shoulders. "He's probably gone, Son."

Charlie hung his head. He held his body stiff so he wouldn't cry. He knew how much work there was to do.

Too much work to take time to look for a stray dog.

CHAPTER
FOURTEEN

Papa put his hand on Charlie's arm.

"He's probably gone," Papa repeated with a slow smile. "But you know, I miss Danny almost as much as you do. And Momma wouldn't mind having a dog around when I go into town. The plowing can wait. Let's see if we can find this pup."

Charlie and Papa tramped through the tall grass calling and whistling. "Lion! Here, boy."

Sometimes they stopped to watch for a rustle in the grass. Charlie wished he could put up his hand and stop the wind, so that he could listen for Lion without its constant singing in his ears.

Overhead the sky was deep blue. Two red-tailed hawks circled slowly, barely moving their wings.

Charlie felt hot and dirty. Papa's shirt was soaked through with sweat, and his face and arms were still covered with soot from the fire.

They searched for the rest of the afternoon.

Papa pointed to the horizon. "Back home at the end of the day, the sun slips behind the birches, oaks, and maples. You never really see it go down. But out here it stays in sight until it sinks below the horizon. You can almost feel the earth turning away from it."

Charlie swallowed hard. "Do you think the wolves will find him, Papa?"

"I don't know, Charlie. I hope not." Papa put his arm around Charlie's shoulder. "Don't forget, lions are known for their courage."

Charlie and Papa searched until the light turned to gold and pink streaks stretched across the sky. They were far from Momma and the wagon, and by the time they saw the flicker of light from the campfire, it was dark.

Charlie moved slowly, his shoulders slumped. Far off, a coyote howled. Charlie shivered at the lonely sound.

Sadie spotted them first. She yelled and raced toward them.

"Charlie, Charlie, where have you been? We thought you were lost!"

Sadie grabbed Charlie's hand and wouldn't let go. She babbled on. "We yelled and yelled but you were too far away. Come, come look."

Charlie stumbled behind her. Sadie led him to a blanket near the fire and pointed proudly. "Look what I found!"

Lion was curled into a ball, sound asleep.

"Lion! But . . . how?" Charlie gasped.

Momma laughed. "Leave it to Sadie Sunshine. She stayed by the chickens while we were fighting the fire, but afterward I went to the creek to bathe . . ."

Ida Jane jumped in. "I was supposed to be watching her. But I was so tired and hot I just closed my eyes for a minute. And that's when Sadie heard the noise."

Sadie nodded, her head bobbing like a little duck. She sat down and patted Lion on the head. "It was a *big* rustle in the bushes, Charlie. I only went a little ways, Momma. I minded you."

Ida Jane said, "Next thing I knew, Sadie had dumped him right on top of me!"

"He likes me, Charlie. Can he be my doggie too?" Sadie begged.

Charlie looked at Papa and held his breath.

Papa's face glowed in the firelight. "Looks to me like Lion already knows he's home."

"I'm heading into Lawrence tomorrow for some supplies," Papa said later, after they had eaten corn-bread and stew made with prairie chicken.

"I hope you bring back some news, James," said Momma with a frown. "I fear the troubles in Kansas are just beginning."

Papa nodded slowly. "Here at Spring Creek we're close to free-soil Lawrence and to proslavery folks in Franklin. If anything happens, we could be right in the middle."

Charlie thought about Flory Morgan, not far away in Franklin. He wondered if he would ever see her again.

Charlie scratched Lion's soft ears. Suddenly he had an idea. "Papa, can you take a letter with you?"

Papa smiled. "Only if you leave me room to write something."

Charlie fetched his journal and tore out a sheet of paper. Momma gave him a pencil and one of her precious envelopes.

"Ask me if you want to know how to spell any-thing," said Ida Jane.

"Write how I found Lion," said Sadie.

Charlie balanced the journal on his knee. Lion curled beside him close.

Dear Grandpa and Danny, Charlie began. *We're starting to make our home in Kansas. We have lots to do before the snows come.*

Charlie looked at his family, sitting together in a circle around their fire. The fire was such a tiny light in the dark, lonely prairie. But above his head friendly stars glittered, just as they had back home.

Grandpa, wrote Charlie, *I think you would like these big prairie skies.*

ABOUT
PIONEER SUMMER

Pioneer Summer is historical fiction. Although Charlie and his family are not real people, I tried to find out as much as I could about family life in Kansas in the 1850s.

To do that, I visited Kansas. I went to the Kansas State Historical Society in Topeka, walked in the Tallgrass Prairie National Preserve near Cottonwood Falls, and went to see some of the important sites during the clashes between "free soilers" and "border ruffians." I also read many books and articles, as well as letters written by people who lived in Kansas during this time. Of course, it's not possible to know exactly what it was like to live in 1855, but I hope this story will make you want to find out more.

Some of the places in the book are real, such as Kansas City and Lawrence. There are several creeks in Kansas called Spring Creek, but I did not have any of them in mind when I placed the Keller family on their claim. One real person mentioned in this book was Eli Thayer. He started the New England

Emigrant Aid Company to help northern families like the Kellers move to Kansas.

As Charlie's father explains, this was an important time in our history. In 1820, the Missouri Compromise was passed. At that time there were eleven slave states and eleven free states. The Missouri Compromise kept a balance between slave and free states by bringing Maine into the union as a free state and Missouri as a slave state. This law also prohibited slavery from being introduced (except in Missouri) north of latitude 36 degrees 30 minutes, which is roughly equal to the southern boundary of Missouri.

The Missouri Compromise lasted for about thirty years. It ended in 1854, when the Kansas-Nebraska Act was passed. The Kansas-Nebraska Act allowed two new territories, Kansas and Nebraska, to be made from land that lay west of the bend of the Missouri River and north of 37 degrees north latitude. It also called for "popular sovereignty" in Kansas and Nebraska. This meant that settlers in Kansas and Nebraska could decide for themselves about slavery. In other words, slavery could be brought into new areas if the people who lived there wanted it. As more people moved to Kansas, conflicts erupted between proslavery and free-state settlers in Kansas. At this time the territory became known as "Bleeding Kansas."

The next two books in the Prairie Skies series, *Cabin in the Snow* and *Our Kansas Home*, explore what it might have been like to live in Kansas at this important time in our country's history through the eyes of Charlie Keller and his family.